HEIDI HECKELBECK
Pool Party!

By Wanda Coven
Illustrated by Priscilla Burris

LITTLE SIMON

New York London Toronto Sydney New Delhi

This book is a work of fiction. Any references to historical events, real people, or real places are used fictitiously. Other names, characters, places, and events are products of the author's imagination, and any resemblance to actual events or places or persons, living or dead, is entirely coincidental.

LITTLE SIMON
An imprint of Simon & Schuster Children's Publishing Division
1230 Avenue of the Americas, New York, New York 10020
First Little Simon paperback edition June 2020
Copyright © 2020 by Simon & Schuster, Inc.
Also available in a Little Simon hardcover edition.
All rights reserved, including the right of reproduction in whole or in part in any form.
LITTLE SIMON is a registered trademark of Simon & Schuster, Inc., and associated colophon is a trademark of Simon & Schuster, Inc.
For information about special discounts for bulk purchases, please contact Simon & Schuster Special Sales at 1-866-506-1949 or business@simonandschuster.com.
The Simon & Schuster Speakers Bureau can bring authors to your live event. For more information or to book an event contact the Simon & Schuster Speakers Bureau at 1-866-248-3049 or visit our website at www.simonspeakers.com.
Designed by Ciara Gay
Manufactured in the United States of America 0520 BVG
10 9 8 7 6 5 4 3 2 1
This book has been cataloged with the Library of Congress.
ISBN 978-1-5344-6128-4 (hc)
ISBN 978-1-5344-6127-7 (pbk)
ISBN 978-1-5344-6129-1 (eBook)

CONTENTS

Chapter 1

SHABBY CHIC

Heidi had a *hairy* problem.

No sooner had she tucked *one* side of her hair into her swim cap than several strands on the *other* side fell out. She stuffed them back in. Then a few more strands spilled over her eyes.

"Oh, merg!" she growled, and pushed those stray hairs back in too. No matter how hard she tried, she couldn't make her hair stay inside that floppy old cap.

"It's all stretched out," Heidi complained.

Mia Marshall, who was in line with Heidi, turned around.

"My cap's baggy too!" Mia said.

Heidi put her finger inside her cap, pulled, and let go. It didn't snap back like a *new* cap. It sagged.

Both girls laughed. Then Mia faced the pool. It was her turn to swim. She pulled on her goggles.

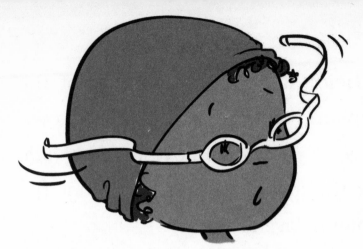

Snap! The strap broke.

"Oh no!" Mia exclaimed. "Now I have to get another pair of goggles!" She ran to the locker room.

Heidi stepped to the edge of the pool and carefully pulled on her own goggles. Then she dove in. *Ahhhhhh,* she thought as she glided through the water. *I love to swim.*

After one lap, Heidi's vision became blurry and her eyes began to sting. *My goggles are leaking!* Heidi thought.

She stopped to empty her goggles. Then she strapped them on and went back to swimming.

Glub! Glub! Glub! More water leaked in as her goggles filled up all over again.

Heidi popped to the surface. Coach
Poole tossed her a pink foam noodle.
"Use this to finish your lap, Heidi,"
Coach instructed.

Heidi leaned on the noodle and began to flutter kick. She moved faster and faster through the water. Just before she reached the wall, the foam noodle cracked in two.

"Not my noodle, too!" called out
Heidi. "The only thing I CAN'T break
is Mia's one-lap record!"

Coach Poole shook her head and
sighed. "It's not you, Heidi," she said.

"That's the second broken noodle today. Our equipment is falling apart!"

The whole team had noticed it. The towels in the locker room had become faded and shabby.

The swim noodles looked like mice had nibbled them. And the kickboards and fins had chips and cracks.

Coach Poole picked up the broken noodle. "Well, run-down equipment can't stop the Little Mermaids!" she declared. Then she blew her whistle.

"Everybody back to work!"

All the girls cheered, except Heidi. *Why do we have to have crummy old equipment?* she wondered. *Maybe there's something we can do . . . ?*

Chapter 2

STICKY WICKETS

"Our swim team's equipment is falling apart," Heidi told her family at breakfast the next morning.

Henry Heckelbeck, Heidi's little brother, stopped sticking chocolate chips into each square on his waffle and looked up.

"Maybe your team should grow gills," he suggested. "Then you would never have to come up for air, AND you'd win every tournament."

Heidi rolled her eyes. "Well, even if we COULD grow gills, we'd still need goggles and swim caps."

"Good point," Henry said as he took a bite of his waffle.

Heidi's fork clattered onto her plate. She couldn't believe Henry agreed with her. Henry *never* agreed with Heidi. She looked at Mom and Dad to see their reaction. Her parents shrugged, and then they all looked at Henry, who was munching his waffle.

"What?" he asked. "Why is everyone looking at me? Do I have chocolate on my face?"

"Oh, never mind," Heidi said, looking at the clock. "It's time to go." She pushed back her chair and grabbed her backpack. "Hurry, or we'll miss the bus!"

Henry slid off his chair—waffle in hand—and followed his sister out the door. The bus had already arrived. They had to run to catch it. Henry stuffed the waffle into his mouth as he ran. Then he flung the crumbs into the bushes outside.

"Enjoy the free food, birds and squirrels!" he yelled.

As they lined up for the bus, Heidi wiped her brow. "Whew! It sure is hot and muggy today!" she complained to her brother, whose cheeks had turned pink.

Henry nodded. "At least it'll be cool on the bus," he said as they clomped up the steps.

Only the bus wasn't cool at all. It felt hotter inside than outside.

Heidi pushed up her sleeves. "Is the AC broken?"

"Yup," the bus driver said as she cranked the door shut.

Heidi groaned and sat down next to her friend Bruce Bickerson. His eyeglasses had fogged up from the heat.

"Wow, it's so sticky and hot out today!" Heidi said. "Sticky wickets!"

Bruce wiped the fog from his glasses with his finger. "Sure wish I had perfected my Chill Choker," he said.

Heidi fanned herself with a notebook and asked, "What's a CHILL CHOKER?"

Bruce popped his glasses back on. "It's a necklace that cools you down when it's hot," he said. "But it doesn't work very well yet. It only makes your neck and ears cold."

"Cool. Well, let me know when you have a breakthrough," Heidi said, and she blew a strand of damp hair out of her face.

The bus rumbled down the street, and a welcome breeze blew through the open windows. Everyone sighed.

Heidi's thoughts drifted back to the Little Mermaids' equipment problem. She opened her notebook and wrote:

Ideas to Raise Money for New Equipment.

Chapter 3

POOF BALL

Lucy Lancaster bounced up and down as she waited for her friends by the bus.

"I thought you'd NEVER get here!" she cried.

"Why? What's going on?" asked Heidi. "And how come you look like you've seen a GHOST?"

Lucy burst into laughter. "Well, only if you mean a really FUNNY ghost!"

Heidi and Bruce looked at each other and shrugged.

"Seriously, what's up?" Heidi asked.

Lucy quickly pointed across the playground. "See for yourself!" she said in between giggles.

Heidi and Bruce looked across the playground. A bunch of students were staring and pointing at a kid hiding behind a black umbrella. Stanley Stonewrecker was standing beside the mystery person.

Heidi had no idea who it was, but she just *had* to find out. She waved to Stanley, and Stanley waved back, so Heidi jogged over.

"What's going on?" she asked him, trying to peek around the black umbrella. "Are you hosting a new student?"

Stanley's mouth opened, but the person holding the umbrella spoke for him.

"NO, Stanley is NOT hosting a new student—*AS IF!*" the voice said angrily.

Heidi stepped back. "I know that voice. Is that Melanie?"

The feet under the black umbrella began to shift.

"Did you come over here to laugh at me too?" the voice asked.

"No," Heidi replied quickly. "I came to see what was going on."

Then the black umbrella slowly turned to reveal Melanie Maplethorpe. Only Melanie didn't look like her normally perfect self. Her pretty blond hair had turned into a giant poof ball!

Heidi gasped. "What happened to your HAIR?"

As soon as Heidi asked the question, the playground became weirdly silent. Everybody watched Melanie to see what she would do.

Would she scream or shout? Would she float away with her umbrella?

But Melanie didn't do any of those things. She simply told the truth.

"It's this weather," she explained. "My hair gets frizzed out and HUGE when it's hot and humid."

"I'm sorry to hear that," Heidi said.

Melanie shrugged. "Well, at least I only have bad hair days when it's hot outside . . . unlike some people, HEIDI HECKELBECK."

Heidi's jaw dropped. She hadn't expected to be insulted, but Melanie had delivered a direct hit.

 With a small huff, Melanie stuck her nose in the air and stalked off as the untamed fluff ball on her head bounced.

"Oh my gosh, Heidi. I am SO sorry," Stanley apologized. "Melanie is having a really BAD hair day."

Heidi frowned. "No kidding! Her hair looks like a giant bird's nest."

No sooner had those words fallen from Heidi's mouth than a bird swooped into Melanie's hair. Melanie screamed, threw away her umbrella, and ran inside.

The crowd laughed.

Even Stanley chuckled, but then he stopped. "I'd better go help Melanie. She can't see well with all that frizz. Talk to you later."

As Stanley ran off, Lucy and Bruce joined Heidi.

Bruce wiped his brow with the back of his hand. "Let's go inside before anything else weird happens, like our shoes melting into goo."

The three friends giggled, then escaped into the cool, air-conditioned school.

Chapter 4

HOT IDEAS

In math Heidi's class worked on dollars-and-cents worksheets. Heidi loved to count money, especially if it was *hers*. Every week she counted what she saved from doing chores. Then, once she reached twenty dollars, she put the money in the bank.

Heidi finished her worksheet before the rest of the class, so she pulled out her notebook. The assignment had given her ideas for how to raise money for her swim team. She jotted them down:

Perform a swim ballet

Belly flop contest

Lemonade stand

Walk neighbors' dogs

Shovel snow

Create a
swimming-pool-finder app

Garage sale

Car wash

Then Mrs. Welli told the students that time was up.

Heidi tore her list out of the notebook. Then she folded it and slipped it into her pocket to share with Mia, her Little Mermaids teammate.

Mia also went to Brewster Elementary. She was in the grade above Heidi, but they had recess at the same time. Heidi would talk to her about it then.

As everyone turned in their work, Mrs. Welli clapped her hands.

"Students, we have a change of plans today," she announced. "Recess will be in the classroom. It's too hot to go outside."

Heidi snapped her fingers. *Merg! I guess I'll have to find Mia AFTER school,* she thought.

At the end of the day, Heidi hurried to the playground, hoping to find Mia. Soon Heidi spied her teammate and waved.

"Hey, Mia!" Heidi shouted. "Over HERE!"

Mia nodded and jogged toward Heidi.

"Oh hey, what's up?" Mia asked.

Heidi pulled out her list and unfolded it.

"I started a list," she explained. "It's a list of ideas on how to raise money for new swim team equipment."

"Cool!" Mia cheered. "Can I see?"

Heidi handed her the list, and Mia read it over.

"Hmm, snow shoveling? It might be hard to do that in THIS weather," Mia said.

The girls giggled.

"I guess I wrote down whatever popped into my head," Heidi said nervously.

"Well, it's an awesome list," Mia said. "I love the idea for an app to find swimming pools. But building an app would be really hard. I don't know how to do it. Do you?"

Heidi frowned and shook her head. Maybe her ideas were not so great.

"I just thought people might want to cool off in this heat wave."

Then Mia's face lit up. "Wait, that's it! What if we threw a pool party for everyone instead of having Little Mermaids practice on Saturday?"

Heidi's eyes grew wide. "I LOVE that idea! We could charge a fee to get in and for snacks and stuff."

Mia nodded and said, "Okay, I'll have my mom talk to Coach Poole and the community center. Hopefully, they will say YES. Oh, this is so exciting!"

The girls high-fived and parted ways to catch their rides home.

As Heidi walked to her bus, everyone around her looked hot and droopy from the heat.

A pool party is exactly what Brewster needs.

Chapter 5

HO-HUM

The next day Heidi's class had recess outside. It was still hot, but the clouds made it feel a tiny bit cooler. Heidi was waiting to play foursquare when she felt a tap on her shoulder.

"Heidi!" said Mia. "Sorry I missed you this morning. My bus was late."

"Did you talk to Coach Poole last night?" Heidi asked.

Mia clasped her hands together. "I did! She LOVES the pool party idea! I already made a sign-up sheet for everything we'll need—snacks like cookies and chips, sandwiches, and more. Just look!"

Mia handed the sign-up sheet to Heidi.

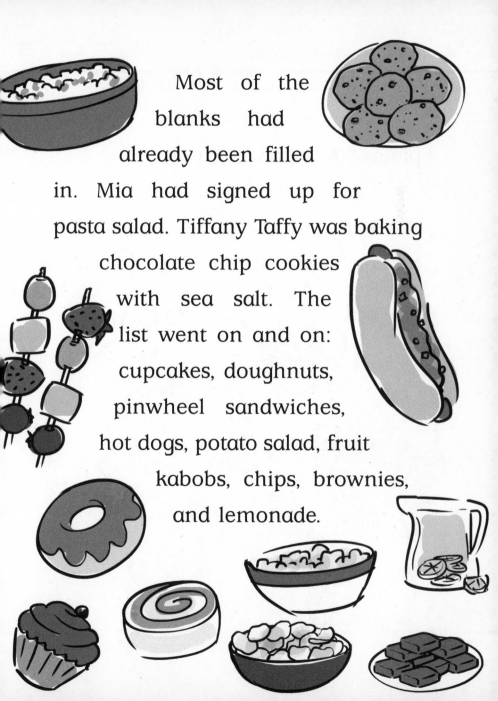

Most of the blanks had already been filled in. Mia had signed up for pasta salad. Tiffany Taffy was baking chocolate chip cookies with sea salt. The list went on and on: cupcakes, doughnuts, pinwheel sandwiches, hot dogs, potato salad, fruit kabobs, chips, brownies, and lemonade.

"How can I help?" Heidi asked.

"Hmm. You could bring cups and plates," Mia suggested.

"I guess so," Heidi mumbled— not knowing quite what to say. She thought cups and plates were ho-hum.

Mia squealed as if Heidi had just said yes. "Thanks, Heidi! That's perfect! This pool party is going to be a blast!"

Then Mia turned and ran back to her classmates.

Heidi grumbled to herself. *Oh, merg-a-doodle-doo! Who cares about cups and plates? It's the stuff ON the plates and IN the cups that people remember!*

She had to think of something else to bring—something *really* fun. Heidi tried and tried, but she couldn't come up with anything that Mia didn't already have on the list.

Maybe I can find something in my Book of Spells, she thought. *There must be a special spell for the perfect pool party treat!*

Heidi couldn't wait to get started.

Chapter 6

THE BIG SECRET

When Heidi got home from school, she went straight to her room and pulled her *Book of Spells* out from under the bed. She thumbed through the pages and found a spell for the one thing every major pool party needed.

Magical Ride-Along Pool Party Float

Have you ever been to a pool party? Perhaps you had to sign up for something to bring, like treats or snacks? Or maybe you had to sign up for something boring, like cups and plates? Well, if you'd like to be the life of the party, then this is the spell for you!

Ingredients:

1 blow-up pool toy

1 sprinkle of glitter

1 splash of water

2 deep breaths out

Sprinkle glitter on top of the pool toy, followed by the splash of water. Then blow two deep breaths out. Hold your Witches of Westwick medallion over your heart and place one hand on the pool toy. Chant the following spell:

Cha-BOOM! BOOM! BOOM!

Cha-BOOM! BOOM! BOOM!

MAKE THIS POOL TOY

Sha-ZOOM! ZOOM! ZOOM!

Heidi copied the spell onto a piece of paper for later. Then she rummaged through her desk drawer and pulled out a tube of pink glitter.

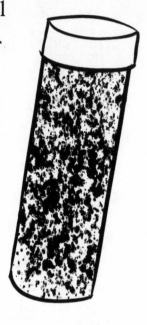

Now all I need is a ride-on pool toy, she thought. *And I know JUST the one!*

Heidi ran down to the garage and unhooked her oversize unicorn float from the wall. It had a golden horn with a rainbow mane, tail, and wings! It even had handles to hold.

She gave the unicorn a big hug and said, "You are going to make a HUGE splash at the pool party! Just you wait!"

By the time Heidi got to school the next day, *everybody* knew about the pool party.

"What are you bringing to the party, Heidi?" Lucy asked. "Your famous Heckelbeck Chocolate Chunk cookies? Or those double chocolate cupcakes with rainbow frosting?"

Heidi shook her head. "Neither," she said. "I'm bringing cups and plates."

Heidi was about to tell her friends about her unicorn surprise, but then Melanie and her giant hair barged into the conversation.

"You're bringing DISHWARE?" Melanie said in her snooty voice. "Well, at least you're not bringing those disgusting cookies you made for the cookie contest. They smelled like old gym socks." Melanie pinched her nose.

Heidi took a deep breath and said, "Well, for your information, I happen to be bringing something MAJORLY MAGICAL to the party."

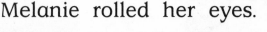

Melanie rolled her eyes.

"Like WHAT?"

Heidi almost told Melanie about the float, but then she realized that's exactly what Melanie wanted her to do.

"Sorry," Heidi said. "It's a secret."

Melanie glared at Heidi. "REALLY?" she said in disbelief. "I'll bet it's only a secret because you don't HAVE anything planned for the party."

Heidi stuck out her chin. "Do too!"

"Then why don't you tell us?" Melanie demanded.

Heidi put her hands on her hips. "I'll only tell you if you promise to go away. And you can't blab my secret all over school, either."

Melanie humphed. Then she said, "FINE. Because believe me, Heidi Heckelbeck, the last person I want to be around is YOU."

Heidi felt her cheeks flush. "OKAY, then I'll tell you!" she said through gritted teeth.

Melanie leaned in closer. Lucy and Bruce leaned in closer too.

"The secret . . . ," Heidi began, "is that I'm bringing a giant unicorn float that will take kids on rides around the pool."

Everyone gasped—even Melanie.

"Wow!" Lucy exclaimed. "That really IS super-cool!"

Bruce nodded. "I'd ride a unicorn."

Melanie just sniffed. "Well, your secret's safe with me," she said, which Heidi didn't believe for one second. "And, PS, you'll still see me in class, HEIDI." Then Melanie walked away.

Heidi turned to Lucy and Bruce.
"That girl is absolutely, POSITIVELY
merg-o-listic!"

And that was all Heidi had to say
about *that*.

Chapter 7

PUMP IT UP!

On the morning of the pool party, Heidi dressed in her pink swimsuit with polka dots and matching shorts.

Before leaving, she stuffed her unicorn float into a large bag. She also tossed in the pink glitter, her medallion, and a bottle of water—everything she would need to perform her spell. She packed the party cups and plates in a separate shopping bag.

Aunt Trudy drove Heidi to the pool. Mom and Dad had gone earlier to set up. Henry had spent the night with his best friend, Dudley, and was coming to the pool later.

Flip! Flop! Flip! Flop! Heidi's sandals slapped the tiles as she walked into the pool area. The grown-ups had set tables filled with platters of food and drinks. Heidi dropped off her cups and plates. Then she hid the float in the storage room.

Just as Heidi stepped out of the
storage room, Mia leaped out with
the rest of the team and cried out,
"Hi, hi, Heidi!"

Heidi was so surprised she nearly jumped out of her flip-flops.

"Oh, hey!" Heidi said as the girls crowded around her. She took a step back.

"When were you going to tell us about your big secret—your float ride?" Mia said. "We can't wait to see it in action! Is it ready yet?"

Now Heidi knew that Melanie had told everyone about the float. She glanced at the clock on the wall. It was nearly party time.

Heidi shrugged. "Um, it'll be ready pretty soon! I promise!"

The girls cheered and headed off to prepare for the crowd.

"Well, let me know if you need any help!" Mia said with a wink.

"Thanks, but I can handle this," said Heidi.

Once she was sure nobody was looking, Heidi quickly snuck back into the storage room. She pulled out the unicorn float along with the glitter, the water, and her Witches of Westwick medallion. *At least, I HOPE I can handle this,* she thought.

Heidi unfolded the directions and carefully followed each step.

Instantly the unicorn began to sparkle and inflate. Heidi watched it grow to full size. Then the unicorn blinked its eyes and spoke.

"Hello! My name is Uni, and I am a magical unicorn float! What can I do for you?"

Heidi put her finger to her lips. *"Shhh.* You can start by keeping it down! Nobody around here has ever heard of a talking unicorn float."

Uni whinnied softly. "Then it'll be our little secret."

"Okay," Heidi agreed with a smile. Then she explained that she wanted the float to give kids rides around the pool.

"The pool party is on the other side of this door," she explained. "I'll clap once to begin the ride. Then give each kid two laps around the pool. And in case of an emergency, two claps will mean stop. Is that okay with you?"

Uni bobbed his colorful horn. "That sounds delightful!"

Heidi hugged the float around the neck. "Then let the pool party BEGIN!"

Chapter 8

WiLD RiDE!

Heidi placed her unicorn float by the edge of the pool. She was ready for the crowd. The food tables were ready too. Coach Poole sat down at the entrance to collect entry fees, and the lifeguards stood poolside. Party time had finally come!

Families swarmed into the pool area. Soon Heidi had a long line for her ride. She clapped her hands, and Uni motored the kids around the pool. The float swerved around swimmers like they were traffic cones.

"My turn!" said Henry, who was next in line. He straddled the unicorn and grabbed hold of the handles. Heidi clapped, and Henry whizzed around the pool. The unicorn left a wake in the water.

"Whoa, I don't remember this unicorn being so much FUN!" Henry said when the ride was over. Then he whispered in Heidi's ear. "It's almost as if it were MAGIC."

Heidi laughed and patted her brother hard on the back.

"Glad you liked it," she said, carefully ignoring Henry's magic comment. Heidi didn't want anyone to get suspicious. "Now, who's next?"

Standing at the front of the line was
Miss Frizzy Monster herself, Melanie.
"I'm next, Heckelbeck. And all I can
say is your SECRET ride better be
worth it."

"I guess you'll have to see for yourself," Heidi said.

With a snort, Melanie jumped onto the float, and Uni almost tipped over.

"Be GENTLE!" Heidi cried.

Melanie ignored her and waited for the ride to begin.

Heidi had a bad feeling about this, but she still clapped her hands. *Whoosh!*

Uni took off around the pool, but Melanie looked unimpressed.

"Heidi's ride is for boring babies!" she announced. "I'll make it exciting!"

Then Melanie tugged hard on the unicorn's neck.

"PLEASE STOP!" Heidi shouted as Uni began to rear and buck like a wild horse.

"Whee!" Melanie hollered as she held on tight.

Everyone watched the wild float. It was impossible not to!

Heidi clapped her hands twice to stop the ride, but Uni could not hear her over Melanie's squeals.

"Oh no!" Heidi gasped.

Had her magic spell just thrown the Little Mermaids' pool party into the deep end?

Chapter 9

POOL PARTY HERO

Clap! Clap!

Ker-splash!

Heidi jumped into the pool with a noodle and flutter kicked fast to the unicorn float. A lifeguard blew her whistle and jumped into the water too.

Heidi had to act quickly if she wanted to keep this party from going down the drain. When she reached the float, she whispered into Uni's ear, "Thank you for everything, but the magical rides are over."

Uni winked at Heidi, and—*ZAP!*—
the float became instantly still as
Melanie lost her grip and flopped into
the pool.

When Melanie bobbed back to the
surface, Heidi handed her a noodle.
"Here, take this."

Melanie grabbed the noodle and took a deep breath. Then she touched her head and screamed, "My HAIR! It got all WET!"

Her shriek echoed off all the walls.

Heidi nodded, then swam her classmate to the edge of the pool.

Coach Poole helped
Melanie out of
the water and
wrapped a blue
towel around
her. Then Heidi
climbed out of the
pool by herself.

"Heidi saved the
day!" Mia shouted.

Everyone clapped and
cheered. And just like
that, Heidi became
a pool party hero.

Chapter 10

CHOW TIME!

Being a hero made Heidi hungry. She fixed a plate that was loaded with a sandwich, potato salad, a fruit kabob, and a cupcake . . . and Heidi ate every bite.

Hmm, if I'm this hungry, then Melanie must be starving! she thought.

Heidi prepared another plate and found Melanie at the far end of the pool. She was hiding in the corner by the fin bin all by herself. Her wet hair curled wildly over the top of her head, and her towel hung over her shoulders like a cape.

Heidi held out the plate of food and a cup of lemonade.

"This is for you," she said.

Melanie smiled. She took the plate and set the lemonade on the floor beside her.

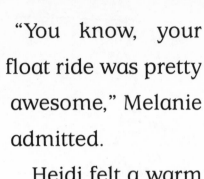

"You know, your float ride was pretty awesome," Melanie admitted.

Heidi felt a warm feeling wash over her. "Thanks," she said. "I'm sorry your hair got wet, but it looks really cool this way, like a rock star."

Melanie shrugged. "You think? I kind of like it too. Maybe I should thank you for giving me a new hot-weather hairstyle."

Heidi laughed and said, "Anytime."

As Heidi turned to go, Melanie called out to her. "Hey, Heidi? Can you tell whoever brought the cups and plates to the party that they did a really good job? It's the PERFECT pool party design."

Heidi blushed because Melanie knew exactly who had brought the dishware.

"Okay," Heidi said, playing along. "I'll let her know."

Suddenly Mia rushed to Heidi's side. She was practically floating like a ball in the water.

"Come with me!" Mia said, tugging her friend by the arm. "Coach Poole is about to make an announcement!"

Heidi waved good-bye to Melanie and joined her other teammates and their coach.

"Thank you to everyone who came out today!" Coach Poole called into her megaphone. "I am thrilled to

announce that the Little Mermaids'
pool party raised enough money to
buy new equipment for the team. To
show our appreciation for your help,
here's a team cheer!"

The guests hooted, hollered, and
clapped loudly.

Then, on the count of three, the Little Mermaids stood up and sang:
"We're the Little Mermaids!
We raised a lot of CASH!
Now the Little Mermaids
will make a BIGGER SPLASH!
GO-O-O-O-O, Mermaids!!!"

The team waved to the crowd and then hugged and playfully ruffled one another's hair.

Heidi squealed with laughter, and when her teammates were done, she had a whole new hairdo . . . that looked just like a bird's nest.

Heidi Heckelbeck and Bruce Bickerson talked about narwhals the whole way to school.

"Narwhals are the unicorns of the sea!" Heidi said as the two friends hopped off the bus. "And they grant wishes with their magical horns!"

Heidi loved these mysterious

An excerpt from *Heidi Heckelbeck for Class President*

whales with the single spiral tusk.

Bruce looked at Heidi as if *she* had a horn. He was a scientist, and scientists love facts.

"There are so many things wrong with that statement," Bruce declared. "First of all, it's not a horn, it's a tooth that grows out of the narwhal's lip. Second, the tooth cannot grant wishes, because the tooth is not magical. Third, and most important, there is no such thing as magic."

Heidi giggled, because of course there was such a thing as magic. She practiced magic all the time! But she

An excerpt from *Heidi Heckelbeck for Class President*

couldn't exactly tell Bruce she was a witch.

"Okay," she challenged, "if you're such a great scientist, how can you say magic doesn't exist until you prove it doesn't exist?"

Bruce laughed loudly, and Heidi was so busy watching him, she forgot to look where she was going.

Sploosh!

She stepped right into a deep puddle. Cold water filled one of her sneakers.